NIGHTMARE MANSION 2

Nightmare Mansion 2

Legacy of Shadows

MATTHEW PETCHINSKY

Apophis Enterprises LLC

~ 1 ~

Nightmare Mansion 2: Legacy of Shadows
By: Matthew Petchinsky

Chapter 1: New Foundations

It was the sort of evening that draped itself over the town of Ravenhill like a dark velvet shroud, the sun dipping below the horizon as if wary of what its absence would usher in. In this town, nightfall was more than a transition from day; it was a deep breath before plunging into a pool of whispered tales and unsolved mysteries.

At the heart of these tales was the Ravenhill Mansion, a structure that loomed at the edge of town, casting long shadows even under the moon's watchful eye. Recently reconstructed after years of abandonment, the mansion stood as a monument to its own haunted past, yet now bore an inexplicably inviting allure.

Liam, Marcus, Eliza, and Sophia were an unlikely quartet, each drawn not by random chance but by a magnetic pull to the mansion's mysteries. Liam, a local historian's son, had grown up on stories of the old mansion's horrors and secrets. His keen interest in the supernatural had always been more scholarly than fearful. Marcus, a newcomer with a penchant for adventure, saw the mansion as a dare, a tangible challenge to be conquered. Eliza, the skeptic, was more interested in disproving the ghost stories that enthralled her friends than in confirming them. Sophia, quiet and introspective, felt a strange connection to the mansion, as if the answers to questions about her mysterious ancestry lay within its walls.

The mansion itself had undergone a transformation that puzzled the elders of Ravenhill. What was once a crumbling relic was now almost aggressively grandiose, with newly polished stone facades and gleaming, unblemished windows that reflected the moonlight with eerie perfection. Its gates, previously rusted and unwelcoming, now stood open, as if inviting passersby to enter.

On this particular evening, the four friends stood at those very gates, each with a flashlight in hand and a backpack slung over their shoulders. The air was crisp, carrying the scent of old leaves and the distant promise of winter. They exchanged glances, a mix of excitement and apprehension flickering in their eyes.

"Looks less like a haunted mansion and more like something out of a fairy tale," Marcus joked, breaking the tense silence.

"Maybe the ghosts got a renovation budget," Eliza quipped, but her humor did little to lighten the mood.

Liam stepped forward, his voice low and serious. "They say the last owner disappeared without a trace—left everything behind. People have heard sounds, seen lights. The stories didn't die with the old mansion."

Sophia, looking up at the towering structure, felt a chill that had little to do with the breeze. "There's something about this place," she murmured, "like it's waiting for something... or someone."

With a collective nod, they pushed through the gates. The path to the mansion was lined with newly planted trees that swayed gently, their leaves whispering secrets. As they approached the heavy oak front door, it swung open silently, as though it had been expecting visitors.

The interior of the mansion was a stark contrast to its gothic exterior. The foyer was bright and welcoming, with polished marble floors and walls adorned with tasteful, modern art. Yet, the house did not surrender its eerie essence. The air inside was cool and carried a faint, unplaceable aroma—like old books forgotten in a damp cellar.

They moved through the ground floor, their footsteps echoing in the vast halls. The living room was furnished with a blend of old and new—antique sofas reupholstered in vibrant, contemporary fabrics, and a grand piano that gleamed under the soft light of modern chandeliers.

It was in the library that they first sensed they were not alone. The shelves were stocked with books that ranged from ancient tomes to recent bestsellers. As Marcus reached out to pull a book from the shelf, a cold draft swept through the room, and a whisper, almost inaudible, filled the air.

"Leave..."

The word hung between them, a soft yet unmistakable intrusion. They froze, turning to each other in silent questioning.

"This is what we came for, isn't it? To find out if the stories are true?" Liam said finally, his voice steady but his hands betraying a slight tremble.

Together, they agreed to press on, their journey into the mansion's heart guided by flickering shadows and the sense that whatever resided within was slowly awakening from its slumber. With each step deeper into the mansion, the air grew colder, the shadows darker, and their resolve more determined.

The legacy of shadows was just beginning to stir.

Chapter 2: Unveiling the Curse

The weight of the mansion's history seemed to press down on the group as they delved deeper into its refurbished corridors. The eerie tranquility that greeted them at the entrance was now replaced by a subtle, unsettling undertone that seemed to whisper from the very walls themselves.

They ventured first into the grand hallway, where the moonlight spilled through large bay windows, casting elongated shadows that danced across the floor. The walls were lined with portraits, their subjects' eyes following every step the group took. The paintings were a timeline of the mansion's past residents, each face framed in ornate gold or dark mahogany, exuding an air of solemnity and secrets long kept.

Marcus paused before a particularly striking portrait of a woman dressed in the garb of the late 18th century, her expression stern yet haunted. "Look at her eyes," he whispered, "It's like she's trying to tell us something."

Eliza, ever the skeptic, scoffed lightly. "It's just a painting, Marcus. Artists aim to capture emotion, not send messages from beyond."

However, Sophia felt a strange pull towards the painting. She moved closer, her eyes locked with the painted woman's, feeling an inexplicable sorrow welling up inside her. "There's something sad about her," Sophia said softly, almost to herself. "As if she's trapped."

Their path led them to a vast library, a room so expansive it seemed to contain the breath of centuries. Here, the modern renovations gave way to the mansion's original character—shelves carved from dark wood reached up to a ceiling lost in shadows, and the air was thick with the scent of leather and old paper.

It was Liam who first noticed the large, leather-bound book resting on a stand in the center of the room. Its cover was embossed with cryptic symbols and a title that read simply, "Legacy of Shadows." The book was thick, its pages edged with gold that flickered in the dim light, as if hinting at the forbidden knowledge held within.

Carefully, Liam opened the book to its first page. The words were written in an elegant, flowing script, but it was the content that made the group draw in a collective breath. The book chronicled the history of the mansion, beginning with its original construction by a reclusive baron who was rumored to dabble in the occult. It spoke of curses cast, spirits bound to the earthly realm, and shadows that moved with a life of their own.

"The baron believed that he could control the spirits he summoned," Liam read aloud, his voice echoing slightly in the large room. "But something went wrong. The spirits turned against him, and his family suffered terrible fates. The mansion was cursed, doomed to be a vessel for the restless spirits forever trapped within its walls."

As they absorbed the tale, a chill ran through the room, and the air thickened. Eliza turned the page, and the group found detailed accounts of various supernatural occurrences documented by previous inhabitants—phantom footsteps, unexplained voices, and apparitions that appeared with the moon's cycle.

Sophia's fingers brushed against a margin where handwritten notes were scribbled. "Look here," she said, pointing. The note was newer, written with a shaky hand, "Beware the heart of the home, for therein lies the key to binding—or unleashing—the curse."

"The heart of the home?" Marcus mused, his brow furrowed. "Could it be talking about the basement? Or maybe there's a hidden room we haven't found?"

They agreed that to understand the full nature of the curse—and perhaps find a way to break it—they needed to explore more of the mansion, particularly the lesser-known areas hinted at in the book. Fueled by a mix of fear and determination, the group decided to press deeper into the mansion's shadowy heart, each step taking them closer to the unseen forces waiting in the obscured corners of the Ravenhill legacy.

As they left the library, the sound of a distant door creaking open halted their conversation. They turned as one, peering down the dark corridor from where the sound emanated. It was an invitation, a challenge, and perhaps a warning—all rolled into one. The adventure was truly about to begin.

Chapter 3: Liam's Challenge

In the dimly lit corridor of the Ravenhill Mansion, the quartet's footsteps echoed ominously as they ventured back toward the library. The air felt denser here, saturated with an ancient quiet that seemed almost sacred. The echo of the creaking door had led them back to this repository of knowledge, now transformed into an arena for an unexpected encounter.

As they re-entered the library, a strange sight awaited them. At the far end of the room, near the grand hearth where shadows played against the stones, sat a figure out of legend—a Sphinx. It was majestic, its leonine body carved from what appeared to be seamless stone that transitioned into the soft flesh of a human from the chest up. Its eyes, a deep and penetrating amber, fixed intently on Liam as he stepped forward.

The Sphinx's presence was as enigmatic as it was startling. It regarded Liam with a curious tilt of its head, its lips parting slightly as if about to speak. The air around them vibrated with a palpable tension, and the others stepped back, giving Liam the floor.

"Seeker of truths, you have come to challenge the shadows of this house," the Sphinx intoned, its voice a melodic blend that resonated through the vast chamber. "Answer my riddles, and I shall grant you the keys to the mansion's deepest secrets."

Liam, his interest in mythology ignited, steadied his nerves and nodded, signaling his readiness. He understood the stakes—mythological creatures such as the Sphinx were known for their merciless penalties for incorrect answers.

"Here is your first riddle," the Sphinx began, its eyes never leaving Liam's. "I speak without a mouth and hear without ears. I have no body, but I come alive with wind. What am I?"

Liam thought for a moment, the answer coming to him from the stories his father used to tell. "An echo," he replied confidently.

The Sphinx's eyes glinted, a small nod affirming his correct answer. "Very well," it continued. "Now for the second riddle: The more of this there is, the less you see. What is it?"

The riddle was simpler, a common one that Liam had encountered in books. "Darkness," he answered without hesitation.

A trace of a smile seemed to touch the Sphinx's lips, and it moved on to the final challenge. "Last riddle: I am not alive, but I grow; I don't have lungs, but I need air; I don't have a mouth, but water kills me. What am I?"

Liam paused, thinking deeper this time. The answer seemed to elude him as he pictured various possibilities. The tension among his friends was palpable, their breaths held in anticipation. Then, it struck him, a simple concept often overlooked. "Fire," he said slowly, hoping his logic was sound.

"Correct," the Sphinx declared, its tone conveying a touch of respect. "You have answered well, seeker. The secrets of this mansion are bound by time and shadow, woven into the very fabric of its existence. Look beneath the surface; seek out the heart where all is bound. The answers you seek about the curse and the fate of those who dwelled here lie hidden in the darkest depths of Ravenhill."

With those cryptic words, the Sphinx's form shimmered, dissipating like sand blown away by a strong wind, leaving behind only the echo of its voice. Liam stood for a moment, processing the Sphinx's advice, his heart racing with the thrill of the encounter and the weight of the task ahead.

Turning to his friends, who approached with looks of awe and concern, Liam shared the Sphinx's guidance. They realized that the mansion was revealing itself to them not just through physical exploration but through challenges that tested their intellect and resolve.

The group gathered their thoughts and prepared to delve deeper into the mansion, specifically aiming to find this 'heart' where secrets lay. They felt a renewed sense of purpose, understanding that the path ahead would demand more than just courage—it required wisdom, unity, and an unyielding pursuit of truth. The journey into the mansion's dark heart was just beginning, and Liam felt ready to lead the way, his resolve fortified by the Sphinx's riddles.

Chapter 4: Riddles of Fate

The echo of the Sphinx's departure lingered in the air as the group ventured deeper into the shadowy corridors of Ravenhill Mansion. With the initial trio of riddles successfully answered, Liam felt a surge of confidence. Yet, the air around them seemed to thicken with anticipation, a silent reminder that the true challenge had only just begun.

They soon found themselves in a less frequented part of the mansion, where the air was colder, and the walls were lined with ancient tapestries that told tales of mythical encounters and battles with beasts. The dim light flickered, as if hesitant to reveal too much.

As they entered a circular chamber, the door shut behind them with an ominous thud. Before them stood the Sphinx once again, its form more imposing than before, bathed in the ghostly glow from the single window overhead. The creature's eyes fixed on Liam, its gaze piercing as it prepared to deliver another set of riddles.

"Seeker, your journey continues," the Sphinx announced, its voice echoing off the stone walls. "But be warned, each failure to solve my riddles will bring you closer to my own fate—bound between the realms of man and beast."

Liam nodded, understanding the gravity of each response he would give. His friends stood back, their faces lined with concern but unable to aid him in this trial.

"Here is your riddle," the Sphinx began, its tail flicking with a rhythm that matched the increasing tension in the air. "I fly without wings, I cry without eyes. Wherever I go, darkness flies. What am I?"

Liam pondered, his mind racing through possible answers. "A cloud," he finally said, his voice less certain than before.

The Sphinx shook its head slowly, and a shiver ran down Liam's spine. Before their eyes, his hands began to morph, his skin stretching and reshaping into a paw-like form with sharp claws. It was subtle at first but unmistakably real. The group gasped, and Liam pulled his hands close, his breath quickening.

"The correct answer was 'smoke,'" the Sphinx clarified, its tone impassive. "Proceed with caution, seeker. Here is your next challenge: I am taken from a mine and shut up in a wooden case, from which I am never released, and yet I am used by almost every person. What am I?"

Liam's mind felt clouded, his recent transformation weighing heavily on him. He struggled to concentrate, the answers slipping like sand through his fingers. "Coal," he guessed, desperation tinging his voice.

Again, the Sphinx's response was a slow, deliberate shake of its head. Another wave of transformation rippled through Liam, his face beginning to elongate, his ears sharpening. The physical changes were terrifying, propelling him into a realm of panic and fear.

"Pencil lead," the Sphinx said softly. "Focus, seeker. Your next riddle is this: I build up castles. I tear down mountains. I make some men blind, I help others to see. What am I?"

This time, Liam took a deep breath, trying to calm his racing heart and focus. The answer came to him from a distant memory of his father discussing various riddles at the dinner table. "Sand," he responded, his voice steadier.

The Sphinx nodded, and for a moment, Liam felt relief wash over him. No further transformation occurred, and he felt a slight easing of the changes that had begun to take hold.

Encouraged but still deeply unsettled, Liam faced the final riddle. "Alive without breath, as cold as death; never thirsty, ever drinking, all in mail, never clinking. What am I?"

Drawing from the same distant memories and his father's love for classic riddles, Liam answered with more confidence, "A fish."

Correct again, the Sphinx acknowledged his success, and some of the transformations began to reverse. Liam felt his hands returning to normal, the elongation of his face receding. However, the threat remained all too real—a few incorrect answers could permanently alter his fate.

With the riddles concluded, the Sphinx faded away, leaving a heavy silence. Liam, shaken but intact, rejoined his friends, who rushed to his side. They embraced him, relief palpable among them.

"Let's find the heart of this mansion," Liam said, his experience having deepened his resolve. "Whatever secrets it holds, whatever curse it bears, we face it together."

As they left the chamber, the weight of their task loomed larger than ever. The riddles were not just tests of wit—they were warnings and guides, shaping their path forward through the enigmatic and treacherous depths of the Ravenhill Mansion.

Chapter 5: Marcus' Descent

As the group moved further into the depths of the mansion, each member seemed to carry their own burden of fear and curiosity. For Marcus, the thrill of the adventure had always been in overcoming physical challenges. However, the Ravenhill Mansion posed a different kind of test—one that seemed to claw at the edges of his mind.

The air grew noticeably colder as they descended a narrow spiral staircase, leading to what appeared to be a forgotten part of the mansion. The stone underfoot was slick with moisture, and faint, eerie whispers echoed through the air, growing louder with each step. It was as though the mansion itself was speaking in hushed tones.

"Can you hear that?" Marcus whispered, stopping to listen. The others paused, straining their ears.

"I hear it," Sophia replied, her voice tinged with apprehension. "It's like... voices."

The whispers seemed to weave around Marcus, words indistinguishable yet insistently pulling him forward. The others followed cautiously, but it was clear that whatever was calling out was focused on Marcus.

They emerged from the staircase into what seemed to be an old, frost-covered garden. Despite the chill, the garden was eerily beautiful, shrouded in a delicate frost that sparkled under the faint moonlight filtering through the high windows. Vines crept up the stone walls, and statues of mythical creatures stood guard among frozen flower beds.

But it was the center of the garden that drew their eyes—a circular clearing where the frost seemed to dance in the air, swirling with a life of its own. Marcus felt a pull towards the center, the whispers growing louder, urging him forward.

"Marcus, be careful," Liam called out, but Marcus was compelled by an inexplicable need to discover the source of the whispers.

As he stepped into the clearing, the temperature dropped sharply, his breath visible in the air. The ground was covered in a thin layer of ice, crunching slightly under his weight. The whispers coalesced into a single, clear voice, chilling not only in temperature but in its ominous tone.

"Seeker of the cold heart, you tread where few dare," the voice hissed, surrounding Marcus. He spun around, searching for the source, but saw only the shifting frost.

Suddenly, from the shadows cast by the statues, figures began to emerge—tall, gaunt creatures with elongated limbs and eyes that glowed with a hungry light. Wendigos, the legends of the north, creatures born from ice and insatiable hunger, now stood in a semi-circle around Marcus. Their presence was both terrifying and mesmerizing.

"You have entered our domain," one of the Wendigos spoke, its voice a chilling echo. "To pass, you must endure the frost of ages. Survive, and you may proceed. Fail, and become one with the ice."

Marcus felt the cold seep into his bones, a frost unlike any winter's chill he had ever known. His resolve was tested not just by fear but by the physical assault of the supernatural cold. Remembering the Sphinx's challenge and Liam's ordeal, Marcus braced himself, focusing on his inner warmth, on thoughts of sunlit days and the heat of exertion—anything to keep the penetrating cold at bay.

His friends watched helplessly from the edge of the clearing, each silently urging him on, their own fears for his safety a tangible thing in the frozen air.

Time seemed to stretch, the minutes dragging as Marcus stood his ground. Finally, as if accepting his resilience, the Wendigos slowly retreated back into the shadows, their figures dissolving into the frost that had summoned them.

Breathing heavily, Marcus staggered back toward his friends, his body trembling from the cold but unbroken. "I'm okay," he managed to say, though his voice was hoarse from the cold air.

Together, they left the garden, the warmth of the mansion's interior a stark contrast to the supernatural cold of the garden. Marcus' encounter with the Wendigos had changed him, the realization that the mansion was not just a place of physical exploration but of deep, spiritual trials.

As they continued their journey through the mansion, each step took them deeper not just into the physical structure but into the mysteries and the very soul of Ravenhill. Marcus, now more than ever, understood that the challenges they faced were about more than courage; they were about understanding the limits of fear and the strength of the human spirit.

Chapter 6: Frost and Fear

The garden's frost lingered on Marcus's skin even as they ventured deeper into the mansion, the chill a ghostly reminder of the Wendigos' haunting presence. The air was thick with the weight of unspoken fears, and Marcus's mind teetered on the edge of understanding the full magnitude of what he had just survived.

As they navigated through a series of winding corridors and descending staircases, Marcus's encounter with the Wendigos seemed to have unlocked a darker aspect of the mansion. The walls whispered not just with cold drafts but with voices that seemed eerily familiar, echoing doubts and insecurities that Marcus had long buried.

Liam noticed the change first. "You okay, man?" he asked, his voice laden with concern. Marcus nodded, but his eyes betrayed a hint of unrest, shadows flickering within them as if reflecting some unseen horror.

The mansion seemed to respond to Marcus's inner turmoil, the atmosphere growing denser, the shadows stretching longer. When they entered an abandoned drawing room, the door shut behind them with an ominous click, sealing them inside.

In the dim light, Marcus's breathing became labored, his eyes darting around the room. The wallpaper, once grand and vibrant, was now peeling, revealing older, darker layers underneath. It was in these shadows that Marcus's test truly began.

The Wendigos, though physically absent, were not done with him. First came the whispers, soft and sibilant, slithering into his ears. "Is he really your friend?" one voice hissed, speaking of Liam. "Or does he see you as just another pawn in his adventures?"

Marcus shook his head, trying to dismiss the voices, but they persisted, growing louder, more insistent. "Why would he care about someone like you?" another taunted. The room grew colder with each word, the frost creeping along the walls, encircling them like a predator stalking its prey.

Images began to manifest in the frost—visions of Liam turning away from him, dismissing him, laughing at him with others. Marcus's heart pounded painfully against his chest, each vision striking a deep-seated fear of abandonment and betrayal.

Eliza, noticing the distress on Marcus's face, moved closer. "Marcus, these are just tricks, meant to scare you. It's not real," she said firmly, trying to break the spell of the haunting visions.

But the Wendigos were merciless. "He's outgrown you, can't you see? You're just a liability," the voices continued, now echoing around the room, bouncing off the walls and burrowing deeper into Marcus's psyche.

Struggling against the rising panic, Marcus closed his eyes, focusing on his breathing, on the memories of genuine moments he had shared with Liam—challenges they had faced together, victories they had celebrated. Slowly, the real Liam emerged in his mind's eye, not the distorted version the Wendigos wanted him to see.

"Enough!" Marcus finally shouted, his voice echoing powerfully through the room. "I know who my friends are. Your tricks won't work on me!"

With a palpable shift in the air, the cold began to recede, and the whispering voices faded into silence. The visions dissolved into mere wisps of frost that melted away on the ancient carpet.

Liam stepped forward, placing a hand on Marcus's shoulder. "We're in this together," he affirmed, his voice steady and sincere. "Don't let this place or anything in it make you think otherwise."

As the group prepared to leave the room, Marcus felt a renewed sense of resolve. The encounter had not only tested his resilience but had also reaffirmed the bonds of friendship that tied him to his companions. With a deep, cleansing breath, he stepped forward, ready to face whatever the mansion—and the Wendigos—might throw at him next.

Chapter 7: Eliza's Vanity

After the harrowing experiences they had each endured within the haunted confines of the Ravenhill Mansion, the group's resolve was deeply shaken but not broken. Each encounter seemed tailor-made to test their fears and desires. For Eliza, who had always maintained a skeptical and pragmatic facade, her personal challenge lay just ahead.

As they ventured through an ornate corridor lined with gilded frames and crystal sconces that threw eerie shadows across the plush carpet, Eliza's pace slowed. Her gaze was caught by a large, ornate mirror set against one wall, separated from the other artworks and emitting a soft, ethereal glow that seemed to beckon to her.

Curiosity overcame her initial caution, and she stepped closer, alone. The mirror, framed in intricately carved mahogany that twisted like vines, was unlike any she had seen before. Eliza peered into the glass, expecting to meet her own skeptical eyes. Instead, she found herself gazing into a vision of a future saturated with acclaim and success.

The reflection did not show the dusty, shadow-laden corridor of the mansion. Rather, it portrayed her standing on a stage, bathed in the bright light of camera flashes. She was older, more refined, and dressed in a flowing gown that glittered under the spotlight. Around her, a crowd cheered, their faces alight with admiration and envy. Above the din, a voice announced her as "Eliza, the world-renowned psychic, uncovering secrets from beyond."

The vision was intoxicating. It played directly into the deep-seated ambitions she had always harbored but rarely voiced—the desire for recognition, for her abilities as a psychic to be validated and celebrated worldwide.

As she stood transfixed, the images shifted, showing her books on psychic phenomena becoming bestsellers, her face on television screens, and her name in illustrious headlines. Each scene was more glamorous and validating than the last.

"Eliza?" Liam's voice broke through her reverie, sounding distant and muffled as if coming from underwater.

She barely glanced away from the mirror. "Just a minute," she murmured, her eyes locked on the visions of grandeur.

Liam approached, concerned. "What do you see?" he asked, peering into the mirror. To him, it reflected only the corridor as it truly was—dull and deserted.

"It's... it's incredible," Eliza breathed, unable to tear her gaze away. "It's everything I've ever wanted. My future."

Liam looked at her, then back at the reflection, seeing nothing but their tired reflections in the dim light. "Eliza, it's not real. You know how this place works—it's showing you what it thinks you want to see."

But the words struggled to penetrate Eliza's enthralled mind. The mirror whispered to her, promising a future filled with everything she desired—as long as she embraced her role as a psychic wholeheartedly.

Sophia and Marcus joined them, observing Eliza's rapt attention to the mirror. "Eliza, we need to keep moving," Sophia urged gently.

Reluctantly, Eliza tore her eyes away, the visions dissipating as she stepped back. The cold truth of the mansion's corridor washed over her, a stark contrast to the warmth of the adoring crowds in her vision.

As they moved away, Eliza's heart was heavy with a mix of disappointment and enlightenment. She realized that the mirror had not just shown her desires—it had exploited them, preying on her vanity and ambition. The encounter was a stark lesson on the dangers of letting her desires cloud her judgment, especially in a place as manipulative as the Ravenhill Mansion.

With a renewed sense of purpose and a more grounded understanding of her own vulnerabilities, Eliza rejoined her friends, ready to confront the mansion's mysteries with a clearer perspective. Her experience with the mirror had not only revealed the depths of her own ambitions but also reaffirmed her commitment to discerning truth from illusion.

Chapter 8: The Basilisk's Gaze

The chilling realization of the mirror's manipulative power lingered with Eliza as the group continued through the dimly lit corridors of the Ravenhill Mansion. The images of fame and success that had so vividly played before her eyes now seemed sinister, a lure crafted by the mansion to ensnare her with her own desires.

As they made their way through an archway leading into a darker, more oppressive part of the mansion, a sudden sharp sound shattered the heavy silence. The group turned just in time to see the ornate mirror that had entranced Eliza cracking, its surface splintering into a web of jagged lines. The air around them thickened, charged with a palpable sense of impending dread.

From the fractured mirror, a new horror emerged. A creature with scales that shimmered with an oily, iridescent sheen slithered out, its body elongating and coiling with serpentine grace. Its eyes, a piercing, unnatural green, fixed immediately on Eliza.

"The Basilisk," Liam whispered, the name barely escaping his lips. Known in legends for its lethal gaze, the Basilisk was a symbol of punishment and retribution for those who dared to succumb to their baser instincts and desires.

Frozen in place, Eliza's heart raced as she met the creature's gaze. The air seemed to crystallize around her, the cold biting into her flesh. She wanted to run, to look away, but the Basilisk's eyes held her captive, a prisoner of her own ambitions reflected back at her.

"Don't look at its eyes!" Marcus shouted, but it was too late. Eliza's body began to stiffen, her movements growing sluggish as the petrifying curse of the Basilisk took hold.

Sophia, thinking quickly, pulled a mirror from her bag and angled it towards the Basilisk, hoping to reflect its gaze back upon itself. The creature hissed, recoiling as its own reflection caught its eyes. It slithered back, momentarily confused, but the damage to Eliza had already been done.

The group watched in horror as Eliza's skin turned to stone, her expression caught in a moment of realization and regret. Her last living reflection had been that of her own petrified ambition—a stark, unyielding reminder of the cost of her vanity.

As the Basilisk retreated into the shattered remnants of the mirror, the air gradually began to warm, the immediate threat dissipating with the creature's departure. The group gathered around Eliza's stone form, their expressions a mix of sorrow and fear.

Liam, his voice thick with emotion, spoke softly, "We need to find a way to reverse this. There must be something in this mansion that can help—some spell or relic. This can't be the end."

Determined now more than ever, they resolved to delve deeper into the mansion's secrets, hoping against hope to find a cure for Eliza. Her petrified form stood as a grim testament to the mansion's power and as a driving force for her friends to confront whatever dark forces lay ahead.

With heavy hearts, they moved forward, the weight of their task never more apparent. The mansion, with its labyrinthine corridors and endless mysteries, seemed to mock their plight with whispers and shadows that danced just out of reach. But driven by loyalty and the memory of Eliza's vibrant spirit, they pressed on, each step a defiance against the darkness that sought to claim them.

Chapter 9: Sophia's Eternal Mistake

As the group ventured deeper into the eerie expanses of Raven-hill Mansion, the weight of Eliza's transformation into stone hung heavily upon them. They moved through the mansion more cautiously now, aware of the grave consequences each supernatural encounter could hold.

In the gloom of the mansion, the dining hall seemed to offer a brief respite. The grand room was elegantly appointed with a long, ornate dining table set with gleaming silverware and crystal glassware that caught the flickering candlelight from the chandeliers above. It was here that Sophia felt a strange pull, an inexplicable draw to the far end of the hall.

As she approached, the figure of a man materialized from the shadows, his presence commanding yet eerily serene. He was dressed in a bygone fashion, his attire reminiscent of the Victorian era, with a tailored coat and a crisp, white shirt that contrasted sharply against his unnaturally pale skin. His hair was neatly styled, and his eyes, a deep, mesmerizing red, seemed to pierce through the dim light, locking onto Sophia's with an intensity that rooted her to the spot.

"Good evening," he said, his voice smooth and enticing. "You seem troubled. Perhaps I can offer some solace?"

Sophia, caught off guard by his sudden appearance yet captivated by his charm, found herself drawn into conversation. He introduced himself as Alexander and listened intently as Sophia shared the trials they had faced within the mansion's walls.

Alexander nodded sympathetically. "This place can be quite overwhelming to the uninitiated. But it also holds secrets of incredible power. Secrets that could, for instance, offer one the gift of eternal life."

Sophia's interest was piqued. The fear of losing her friends, coupled with the recent loss of Eliza, had left a void in her, a fear of mortality and the fragility of human life.

"Eternal life?" she echoed, both skeptical and intrigued.

"Yes," Alexander continued, his gaze never wavering. "I am much older than I appear, preserved by the very secret I just mentioned. I am a vampire, and I have lived through centuries unscathed by time or disease."

The revelation should have frightened Sophia, driven her away, but the allure of eternal life, the possibility of evading death's inevitable reach, was tantalizing. "And you can share this... gift?" she asked, her voice a mix of doubt and desire.

"I can," Alexander affirmed. "But it comes with a price, as all powerful gifts do. You must be willing to leave your old life behind, to embrace a new existence bound by the night."

The offer dangled before Sophia like forbidden fruit. The thought of living through the ages, of protecting and perhaps eventually reuniting with her petrified friend, seduced her rational mind.

Caught in a whirlwind of emotion and the persuasive charm of Alexander, Sophia consented. "Yes, I'll do it," she whispered, a mix of fear and excitement coursing through her veins.

Alexander's smile was both triumphant and tragic as he leaned in, his fangs bared. The bite was sharp, a searing pain that gave way to a cold that spread through Sophia's body. As the transformation took hold, the room spun, the candles blurred into streaks of light, and Sophia felt herself slipping into a darkness that echoed with distant, haunting laughter.

When she awoke, the dining hall was empty. Alexander was gone, and in his place, a profound solitude enveloped her. Sophia quickly realized the gravity of her choice. Immortal she might be, but the cost was a perpetual separation from the human world she knew, a spectral existence bound not by the love of friends but by the shadows of eternal isolation.

Regret washed over her as she left the dining hall to find her friends, her heart heavy with the knowledge of her irreversible decision. Her steps were silent, her presence barely perceptible, a ghost among the living, doomed to walk the shadows of the world forever changed, forever apart.

Chapter 10: The Feast of Shadows

The grandeur of the dining hall had vanished, leaving Sophia in a state of cold, desolate realization as she slowly comprehended the irreversible choice she had made. The candlelight that once flickered warmly now cast long, menacing shadows across the room, mimicking the chilling transformation within herself. Her senses were heightened, yet her heart was muted, a slow, dull throb that marked the remnants of her fading humanity.

The once-inviting echo of eternal life now rang hollow in Sophia's ears. Alexander, the vampire, had vanished as mysteriously as he had appeared, leaving her alone with her newfound existence. The promise of immortality, which had seemed so rich with possibility, now revealed its true nature—a curse rather than a gift.

As the initial shock of her transformation settled, Sophia felt a gnawing emptiness begin to take root. Her body no longer felt like her own; it was something foreign, something borrowed and not given. She touched her neck where Alexander had bitten her, the site still tingling with a phantom pain that seemed to pulse with a dark reminder of her fate.

Driven by a desperate need to understand what had become of her, Sophia wandered from the dining hall into the mansion's network of shadowed hallways. Each step was a betrayal of her former life, each breath a whisper of the life she had once known. She realized now that the immortality offered by the vampire was not a continuation of life but rather an enduring suspension between life and death.

As she moved through the mansion, Sophia's thoughts turned to her friends. She feared facing them, feared having to explain the choice she had made and the creature she had become. Yet, the bond that tied them together, strengthened by their shared trials within the mansion, drew her inevitably back to their side.

Sophia found them in the mansion's library, a room heavy with the scent of ancient books and secrets. They turned as she entered, their faces etching a mix of relief and concern.

"Sophia, where have you been?" Liam asked, his voice laden with worry.

She approached them slowly, her movements graceful yet unnerving. "I made a mistake," Sophia began, her voice a haunting echo of its former warmth. "I met someone, a vampire. He promised me eternal life, but it was a lie. There's no life in what I've become. I'm trapped in a perpetual shadow, neither alive nor truly dead."

The group listened, horror and sadness washing over them as they took in the full extent of Sophia's transformation. Marcus stepped forward, his expression one of resolved courage. "We're going to fix this," he declared, though his voice trembled with the uncertainty of the promise.

Eliza, still stone and silent, seemed to echo back at them the gravity of their situation—each had faced their own darkness within the mansion's walls, and now they faced Sophia's.

"We need to find Alexander," Sophia insisted, her new, eerie eyes scanning the room as if she could see through the very walls. "He knows how to reverse this. There must be a way."

Their mission was clear, yet daunting. The mansion was no longer just a place of haunted corridors and ghostly whispers; it had become a battleground for their very souls.

Together, they left the library, their determination fueled by the necessity to save Sophia, to bring back the friend they knew and loved. They moved deeper into the mansion, each step a challenge against the darkness, each breath a defiance against the Feast of Shadows that had claimed Sophia. As they ventured forth, the mansion seemed to watch, its ancient walls whispering secrets only the night could understand, secrets they were now bound to uncover.

Chapter 11: Liam's Transformation

The once-sturdy bonds of friendship and shared purpose that had united the group began to fray as the Ravenhill Mansion continued to exact its toll, each room and corridor laying bare more than just the physical architecture of the place, but also the dark spiritual forces it harbored. Liam, who had always felt a connection to the lore and history of the mansion, found himself increasingly isolated in his thoughts, burdened by the responsibility to lead and protect his friends.

Their quest had brought them back to the heart of the mansion —the vast library where Liam had first encountered the Sphinx. The air was thick with the musty scent of old leather and wood, a smell that seemed to saturate the very soul with a sense of ancient secrets and forgotten truths. The library was a labyrinth of knowledge, its walls lined with books that whispered tales of the arcane and mysterious.

Liam stood before the Sphinx once again, its enigmatic presence as imposing as ever. The creature's eyes glowed with an otherworldly light, casting eerie shadows across the rows of books. "Welcome back, seeker," it intoned, its voice resonating deep within Liam's mind.

"I am ready for your final riddle," Liam declared, though his voice betrayed a hint of trepidation. The previous encounters had left marks on him, both physically and spiritually, and he knew the stakes were higher than ever.

The Sphinx regarded him with an inscrutable gaze before speaking, "This thing all things devours: Birds, beasts, trees, flowers; Gnaws iron, bites steel; Grinds hard stones to meal; Slays king, ruins town, And beats high mountain down. What is it?"

Liam paused, his mind racing through possibilities. He thought of legends and myths, of the natural world and the supernatural. Yet, the answer eluded him, slipping through his grasp like sand through fingers.

Time seemed to stretch into eternity as Liam wrestled with the riddle. Finally, he spoke, his voice uncertain, "Is it... time?"

A profound silence followed. The Sphinx closed its eyes, and when it reopened them, the glow had vanished, replaced by a depthless sorrow. "Incorrect," it said softly. "The answer is time, yes. But your answer came too late. The riddle was not just in the asking, but in the timing of the answer."

Liam felt a cold dread wash over him. He had known the answer, yet he had hesitated, doubted his instincts. And now, the price of that hesitation was exacted swiftly.

The transformation began at once. Liam's feet rooted to the spot, his body stiffening as a strange alchemy took hold. His skin turned to stone, starting from his feet and creeping upward, each inch a prison cell locking him in place. His friends watched in horror, helpless to intervene as Liam's form solidified, his expression caught between realization and resignation.

As the transformation completed, Liam stood motionless, a statue among many in the library. His final expression was one of profound sorrow mixed with a scholar's resolve, a testament to his journey and sacrifice.

Marcus, Sophia, and the remaining friends gathered around Liam's stone form, each grappling with the loss. "He's become part of the mansion's collection," Marcus said, his voice choked with grief. "Just like the others we've seen... forever bound to these cursed grounds."

Sophia, her eyes reflecting a sorrow only her immortal sight could fully perceive, added softly, "He sought knowledge and understanding, and now he remains among the greatest collection of mysteries and tales. In some way, it is tragically fitting."

The group stood in silent vigil, the weight of their quest heavier upon their shoulders. The mansion had claimed one of their own, transforming him from seeker to guardian, from flesh to stone.

With heavy hearts, they left the library, knowing that their journey had to continue. Liam's sacrifice was both a caution and a catalyst. They needed to find a way to reverse the curses and liberate their friends, to prevent the mansion from consuming them all. The path forward was fraught with danger and sorrow, but they were determined to fight on, for Liam, for Eliza, and for any hope of breaking the mansion's dark legacy.

Chapter 12: Marcus' Last Stand

The atmosphere within the Ravenhill Mansion had grown palpably thicker with despair following Liam's transformation. Marcus, bearing the brunt of the sorrow and the weight of leadership, found himself reeling under the enormity of their losses. His mind, once filled with strategies and plans, now echoed with the haunting images of his friends—Eliza, forever petrified in stone, and Liam, a silent sentinel in the library.

The rest of the group sensed Marcus's growing unease and despair, but his decision came abruptly, a desperate bid for escape or perhaps a moment of madness driven by overwhelming grief. "I can't stay here," he declared one evening, his voice breaking. "Not with Liam and Eliza like this... and what if the rest of us—"

Sophia tried to reason with him. "Marcus, we need to stick together. We can find a way to—"

But Marcus was already moving, his determination a palpable force as he stormed away from the group, heading towards what he believed to be the mansion's main entrance. The mansion, however, had other plans. Corridors twisted unexpectedly, familiar rooms rearranged themselves disorientingly, and every door he opened seemed to mock his efforts to leave, leading him not outside but further into the mansion's heart.

Exhausted and mentally tormented, Marcus found himself inexplicably drawn back to the frost-covered garden, the place of his initial supernatural encounter with the Wendigos. As he stepped into the icy garden once again, the air around him dropped in temperature, a familiar chill that sank deep into his bones.

The garden, under the cloak of night, was bathed in moonlight, casting long shadows across the frostbitten ground. The statues of mythical creatures that once merely adorned the garden now seemed to watch him with eyes full of dark intent.

He heard them before he saw them—the Wendigos. Their whispers floated through the cold air, a cacophony of voices that spoke of despair and inevitability. "You cannot escape your fate," they hissed, their forms materializing from the icy mist, more numerous than before.

Marcus, realizing the futility of flight, turned to face them. His breath formed clouds of vapor as he spoke, his voice firm despite the shaking of his limbs. "Then let's end this," he challenged, though his heart sank with the knowledge of what that meant.

The Wendigos circled, closing in as the temperature dropped further, a supernatural cold that seeped into Marcus's very soul. He felt the cold gnawing at him, a physical pain that matched the ache in his heart. Images of his friends—Liam's resigned eyes, Eliza's frozen gaze—flashed before him, fueling a brief flare of rage and defiance.

As the cold overcame him, Marcus's last thoughts were of regret and a fierce hope that his friends would find a way to break the mansion's curse. His vision blurred, the figures of the Wendigos merging with the icy garden until all he could see was white.

When the others found him hours later, Marcus was no longer moving, his body encased in a sheath of frost that glimmered under the first light of dawn. The garden was silent, the Wendigos gone as if satisfied with their conquest.

Sophia, tears forming ice on her cheeks, whispered a goodbye to Marcus, her heart breaking for the friend who had tried to protect them to the very end. The group gathered around, their resolve hardened by the sight of Marcus's icy tomb.

The mansion had taken much from them, but they vowed to continue, to fight against the shadows and free their friends from their cursed fates. Marcus's last stand, though tragic, ignited a fire within them, a burning need to confront whatever darkness awaited and reclaim their lives from the grips of Ravenhill Mansion.

Chapter 13: Echoes in the Stone

In the hallowed corridors of Ravenhill Mansion, where whispers of the past mingled with the sighs of the present, the stone figure of Eliza stood as a silent sentinel of sorrow. Frozen in time by the Basilisk's cruel gaze, her form captured the very essence of horror and finality—a testament to the mansion's merciless grasp on those who dared uncover its secrets.

The room where Eliza stood was dimly lit, the light filtering through dust-laden curtains casting eerie patterns on the walls. Her expression, caught in the last moment of human sentiment, reflected a mixture of awe and terror, a poignant reminder of her final realization and regret. The details of her petrification were excruciatingly precise—the folds of her clothes, the strands of her hair, and the haunting clarity in her eyes, all preserved in stone.

Nearby, the Basilisk, the architect of her fate, lay coiled. Its body was a tapestry of scales that shimmered with an otherworldly hue, blending into the shadows of the room. It watched over its petrified prize with eyes that glowed faintly, a guardian of both treasure and tomb.

The air in the room was thick with a palpable sense of loss and resignation. The stone figure of Eliza not only served as a stark reminder of the dangers that lurked within the mansion but also as a beacon of unresolved ambition and thwarted potential. Her friends, when they visited, could not help but feel the weight of her unfulfilled dreams, her silenced voice echoing in the stone contours of her face.

Sophia, now forever changed, felt a deep connection to Eliza's fate. With her new immortal senses, she perceived not just the visual horror but also the residual emotions that clung to the stone figure. She heard the faintest whispers of Eliza's last thoughts, trapped within the marble—the echoes of a vibrant spirit caught in perpetual stasis.

As the group stood around Eliza, they spoke softly, sharing memories of better times, their voices a mixture of defiance and mourning. They discussed plans to counter the mansion's curses, each strategy punctuated by glances at the silent figure that reminded them of the cost of failure.

The Basilisk's presence was a constant reminder of the stakes. Every so often, its eyes would flicker, and its tongue would taste the air, as if savoring the despair that hung around its prize. Its silent watch was a challenge to the group, a dare to continue their quest in the face of such potent adversary.

Determined to not let Eliza's fate be in vain, the group fortified their resolve. They poured over old tomes and grimoires found in the mansion's extensive library, searching for any clue or spell that could reverse the petrification. Each discovery, each small victory in their research, was shared with Eliza's statue, as if in hope that she could still hear them, could still be a part of their journey.

As the days turned into weeks, the room with the stone figure became a sanctuary of sorts, a place where determination was renewed and plans were forged. The Basilisk, ever watchful, never interfered directly again, but its silent presence was a constant psychological pressure, a reminder of the thin line between discovery and destruction.

"Echoes in the Stone" thus captured not only the horror of Eliza's fate but also the enduring impact of her spirit. Her petrified form, both a warning and a motivator, drove her friends to push harder against the shadows of the mansion. And amidst the grief and the battles, her memory remained a powerful echo, shaping their resolve, guiding their steps, and reminding them that even in silence, there can be strength, and even in stone, there can be hope.

Chapter 14: Darkness Consumes

The halls of Ravenhill Mansion, already thick with the scent of decay and ancient dust, now pulsed with a more sinister undercurrent. Sophia, once the heart of the group, driven by a thirst for knowledge and a compassion that tied her friends together, had become something else entirely—a creature of the night, lost to the very darkness she once sought to understand.

In her new form, Sophia had ventured away from her remaining friends, exploring the shadowed corners of the mansion with a newfound grace and a terrible loneliness that clung to her like a shroud. Her transformation at the hands of Alexander, the vampire, had left her estranged not just from her humanity but from the companionship that had once defined her.

As she moved through the mansion's sprawling corridors, the pull of her new instincts led her deeper into areas unexplored by the group. The mansion, sensing her change, seemed to welcome her with open arms, its doors creaking open to reveal hidden rooms and forgotten passageways.

One such passage led her to a grand, dilapidated ballroom, its once opulent decorations now tarnished with age and neglect. The chandeliers hung low, their crystals dulled by years of disuse, and the air was heavy with a silence that spoke of centuries.

It was here that the others found her—the other vampires, the kin of Alexander. Like shadows detaching from the walls, they emerged, their forms sleek and their eyes glinting with a predatory gleam. Sophia, feeling the kinship of her new nature, did not flee. Instead, she stood her ground, the last vestiges of her human emotion battling the cold, eternal hunger that now defined her existence.

The leader of the vampires, a tall figure with hair as black as the void, approached her. His voice was a velvet caress, a dangerous lullaby that spoke of acceptance and belonging. "You are one of us now," he whispered, his eyes locking onto hers. "Come, join the feast of eternity."

Sophia, caught between the remnants of her past life and the dark allure of her new existence, hesitated. Her heart, though no longer beating, ached with a pain that was both sweet and terrible.

The decision was taken from her in the end. The vampires, driven by a hunger as old as time, closed in. The ballroom, once a place of laughter and light, became a theater of horror as they descended upon her. The feast was a gruesome ballet of shadows and whispers, of sharp fangs and softer flesh. Sophia, overwhelmed by the sheer force of her kindred, was consumed not just physically but spiritually, her essence dissolving into the dark tapestry of the vampire lineage.

The vampires left as silently as they had appeared, leaving behind nothing but the faintest trace of their presence, a reminder of the deception that had lured Sophia to her doom. The ballroom, once again silent, held no echo of her struggle—only the lingering scent of ancient blood and a darkness that seemed to sigh with satisfaction.

Back in their makeshift sanctuary, her friends discovered Sophia's absence too late. The realization of her fate, pieced together from whispered legends and the grim evidence in the ballroom, was a blow from which they could scarcely recover. Her end marked not just the loss of a friend but the completion of the vampire's deception, a grim chapter in the tale of Ravenhill Mansion that none of them would ever forget.

As they gathered, the weight of their losses pressing upon them, the mansion seemed to settle around them, its appetite momentarily sated. But the fight was not yet over, and the darkness that had consumed Sophia was a stark reminder of the stakes for which they now played. Her memory, tinged with both fondness and horror, would fuel their resolve to confront the mansion's master and end its legacy of shadows once and for all.

Chapter 15: The House Awakens

The eerie stillness that had once pervaded Ravenhill Mansion was now gone, replaced by an almost palpable sense of anticipation, as if the house itself were gathering strength from the tragedies that had unfolded within its walls. Each room, each corridor seemed to thrum with a life force that was not its own, imbued with the essence of those who had fallen victim to its dark allure.

The mansion, with its labyrinthine layout and countless secrets, had long been a predator in its own right, cunning and insatiable. The demise of Sophia, Liam, Marcus, and Eliza had not been mere endings but fuel for the mansion's own sinister form of renewal. As each had succumbed to their fate—turned to stone, lost to the cold, or consumed by shadows—their life force had not dissipated but had been absorbed by the mansion, their spirits now woven into the very fabric of the structure.

In the aftermath of these losses, the mansion seemed to pulse with a renewed vigor. The walls appeared less decrepit, the air less musty. Even the shadows seemed sharper, as if newly inked by darkness. It was as though the mansion was breathing again, drawing breath from the lives it had extinguished.

The remaining members of the group—now diminished and utterly heartbroken—could feel this transformation. As they moved through the halls, they sensed a change in the atmosphere, a chilling indication that their friends' sacrifices had been co-opted into something far beyond mere death.

In the grand foyer, where the adventure had so innocently begun, the marble floor now gleamed unnaturally under the chandeliers whose light seemed to burn brighter than before. The staircase, once creaking and decrepit, now ascended with a menacing grace, each step polished to a reflective sheen that seemed to mock the survivors with visions of what had been and what could never be again.

The library, where Liam had been transformed, now echoed with a subtle whispering that wasn't just the rustling of ancient pages but seemed to be a murmuration of voices, a chorus of the captured souls. The books themselves vibrated with a newfound energy, as if eager to share the stories they now contained—stories of the fallen, their dreams, their struggles, their ends.

Outside, the garden where Marcus had faced his final moments, the frost had receded, giving way to verdant growth that twisted around the statues and benches with unnatural vitality. The plants seemed to feed on an unseen nutrient, lush and darkly vibrant, as if watered by the despair and demise of those who had trod their paths.

And in the corners of rooms, shadows gathered like spectators, whispering and shifting restlessly. They seemed to be waiting for something—or someone. It was clear to those who remained that the mansion was preparing, rebuilding its strength for the next unwitting souls who would cross its threshold, lured by tales of mystery and the macabre.

In a hidden room, deep within the mansion's heart, the true extent of its awakening was evident. Here lay a tableau of the mansion's making: miniature representations of each room, each meticulously detailed and pulsing with a faint light. A shadowy figure moved among the tableaus, its form blurred and shifting, touching each scene with hands that drew threads of light from one to another, weaving a tapestry of fate and fear.

The surviving group, witnessing this, understood with a grim clarity the role they had played in this renewal. They were not just victims; they were catalysts in the mansion's grand design, their friends now part of the foundation that would lure new victims into the mansion's embrace.

As they left the hidden room, a resolve settled over them, borne of desperation and a fierce desire to not let their friends' essences be trapped in perpetuity. They would find a way to break the cycle, to release the spirits intertwined with the mansion's very stones, or perish in the attempt. For now, they knew, the house was awake, and it was hungry for more.

Chapter 16: Legacy of the Cursed

As the dusk settled into the crevices of Ravenhill Town, a gentle mist began to rise, shrouding the path that led to the imposing structure of Ravenhill Mansion. From afar, the mansion appeared rejuvenated, its once decrepit facades now restored to an eerie semblance of grandeur. Its windows glistened under the waning light of the sun, reflecting a welcoming glow that seemed almost too perfect, too inviting. The grounds, once overgrown and wild, were now manicured with precision, each blade of grass and each hedge sculpted with meticulous care.

The mansion stood silent on the hill, its presence more dominating than ever, a beacon for those drawn to the supernatural, to the tales of hauntings and unexplained phenomena that had circulated in hushed tones across the country. It was these rumors, embellished and twisted through countless retellings, that had attracted a new group of visitors to its doors.

A minivan pulled up along the gravel drive, its tires crunching softly in the quiet of the evening. The occupants, a mix of thrill-seekers and paranormal enthusiasts, disembarked with a sense of eager anticipation. Cameras hung from their necks, and their eyes were bright with the thrill of adventure. They were a diverse group, each member fueled by a blend of curiosity and bravado, unaware of the true nature of the mansion that awaited them.

As they approached the grand entrance, the lead door swung open silently, as if ushered by an unseen hand, inviting them into the foyer that gleamed with deceptive warmth. Inside, the air was perfumed with the faint scent of roses, a fragrance that seemed at odds with the mansion's somber history.

The interior of the mansion was a masterpiece of restoration. The walls were adorned with opulent wallpaper, and the floors boasted polished wood that echoed softly under their steps. Portraits of individuals, presumably former residents, lined the walls, their eyes following the visitors with an intensity that sent shivers down their spines.

"Can you believe this place was once said to be a ruin?" one visitor whispered to another, her voice a mix of awe and disbelief.

"Hard to imagine anyone not wanting to live here," another replied, taking in the grand staircase that spiraled upwards into shadowy recesses above.

As they ventured deeper, exploring the main hall and the library filled with ancient books, their laughter and exclamations reverberated through the halls, stirring the dormant energies of the house. Unseen by the visitors, wisps of shadows flitted along the edges of the rooms, the remnants of past tragedies watching, waiting.

Upstairs, the master bedroom doors were ajar, revealing a suite bathed in the soft light of the setting sun. The beds were made with crisp linens, and a fire crackled merrily in the hearth. It was all too welcoming, too perfectly staged.

As the group dispersed to explore various parts of the mansion, each room seemed to tell a part of the mansion's storied past, yet none revealed the true depths of its darkness. In the dining hall, the table was set for a feast, complete with gleaming silver and crystal glasses that caught the fading light.

Outside, the garden paths beckoned, leading to statues and fountains that appeared serene under the twilight sky. But the true essence of the mansion lay in wait, veiled beneath its restored beauty, its legacy of curses hidden in plain sight.

Back in the shadows of the foyer, the front doors swung shut with a definitive thud, the echo of the lock turning a soft but final click. The visitors, now entrapped in the mansion's embrace, continued unaware of the doors sealing their fate, drawn deeper into the legacy of the cursed, into a night that promised revelations and horrors alike.

And so, the cycle began anew, the mansion's appetite for souls undiminished, its halls once again alive with the footsteps of the unsuspecting, each step a note in the symphony of whispers that was Ravenhill Mansion's eternal song.

Chapter 17: Whispers of the Past

In the newly awakened Ravenhill Mansion, the air thrummed with an energy that was both seductive and sinister. As the new group of visitors wandered the grand halls and explored the labyrinthine corridors, they remained blissfully unaware of the mansion's macabre history and its insatiable hunger. Yet, as they delved deeper, the very fabric of the mansion seemed to resonate with echoes of those who had once fought and fallen within its walls.

The whispers began softly, almost imperceptibly, a gentle murmur indistinguishable from the rustle of the wind through the cracked windows or the creak of the old wooden floors. But as night deepened, these murmurs coalesced into clearer voices, each carrying the weight of untold stories and tragic ends.

In the library, where Liam had last stood, his voice now joined the rustling of the pages. Those who paused long enough could hear faint dictations, snippets of historical lore and cryptic warnings, woven between the lines of ancient texts. "Beware the guardians of knowledge," an airy whisper would caution, the words dissipating as quickly as they formed.

Eliza's presence was most palpable near the stone garden where her fate had been sealed. Here, the cold marble of her statue seemed to pulse with a residual life force. Visitors occasionally felt compelled to stop and stare, drawn by a palpable sense of awe and dread. Whispers here were echoes of ambition and power, a soft lament for potential forever petrified. "Ambition untamed leads to eternal stillness," her voice would sigh through the leaves, a sorrowful reminder etched in the wind.

Marcus, who had braved the cold embrace of the Wendigos in the garden, left a chill in the air that was felt by all who dared wander the frost-touched paths. His laughter could sometimes be heard on the breeze, a sound that was both warm and warning. "The cold reveals our true essence," he would whisper, his voice mingling with the rustling of frozen branches and the shivering of leaves.

Sophia, transformed and ultimately consumed by the shadows of her new kin, infused the mansion with a haunting melancholy. Her whispers were the softest, heard only in the deepest parts of the night when the dark was almost tangible. "Eternity lies not in the days, but in the moments," she would murmur, her voice a velvet shadow that danced along the edges of darkness, urging those who listened to cherish the light.

Together, these voices became part of the mansion's eternal whispering, a chorus that filled the corridors with an unseen presence. They were not just remnants of the past but active participants in the mansion's ongoing saga, their fates a lure to those drawn to the mystery and allure of Ravenhill.

As the new visitors settled into the night, each drawn by their own reasons to the mansion, the whispers grew bolder, crafting an invisible tapestry of allure and terror. The mansion, feeding off their fears and fascinations, seemed to grow stronger, its walls pulsing with captured energies, its shadows deepening.

Unseen by the visitors, the whispers guided them, weaving around their thoughts, planting seeds of doubt and curiosity. Some heard these voices as mere figments of their imagination, rational explanations at the ready. Others felt a deeper connection, a resonance that tugged at their souls, urging them to look closer, to delve deeper.

As dawn approached, and the first light crept through the stained-glass windows, casting kaleidoscopic patterns on the dusty floors, the voices faded into the walls once more. The mansion settled, its hunger temporarily sated, its whispers lying in wait for the next night, when the cycle would begin anew. Each echo in the stone, each breath of the past, served to preserve the legacy of Ravenhill Mansion—a legacy of endless cycles of allure and terror, forever whispered within the ancient walls.

Chapter 18: The Cycle Continues

The first light of dawn, which painted the sky in hues of pink and gold, had barely retreated when the new visitors crossed the threshold of Ravenhill Mansion. As the grand doors closed behind them with a resonant thud, the sense of isolation from the world they knew became immediate and complete. The mansion, rejuvenated and seemingly benign, welcomed them with open arms and veiled threats, its every creak and whisper part of the intricate dance of doom.

The group, a collection of amateur paranormal investigators and thrill-seekers, had come prepared with gadgets and cameras, eager to document what they believed to be mere ghost tales and eerie occurrences. Little did they know, their fates were already woven into the tapestry of the mansion's dark history, sealed by the very spirits that haunted its halls.

As they dispersed to explore, each corner of the mansion seemed to pulse with life. The Sphinx, a relic of a forgotten time now reborn through the mansion's malevolent energies, awaited in the depths of the library. Its laughter echoed through the labyrinth of books, a sound both inviting and mocking. As the group ventured closer, drawn by curiosity, the Sphinx's riddle was posed once more, its answer a key to survival or a step towards doom.

Meanwhile, in the frost-touched garden, the air grew inexplicably colder. The Wendigos, spectral entities born from the mansion's embrace of Marcus's last chilling moments, howled softly, their cries like the wind weaving through frozen branches. Unseen, they stalked the visitors, their presence a palpable force that tugged at the edges of sanity.

Elsewhere, in the shadowed corridors, the Basilisk lay in silent wait. Its cursed gaze had once petrified Eliza, and now it sought new victims, its stare as fatal as the ambitions that had led to Eliza's downfall. The unsuspecting visitors, captivated by the mansion's deceptive beauty, wandered ever closer to their stone fates.

And in the darkest part of the mansion, where the light of day seemed forbidden to enter, the vampires whispered. Their voices, remnants of Sophia's tragic end, mingled with the night air, enticing the visitors with promises of secrets hidden in the shadows. Each whisper was a thread pulling the visitors deeper into the web of the mansion's eternal hunger.

As night fell, the mansion came alive with the symphony of its cursed inhabitants. Laughter, howls, silent stares, and enticing whispers filled the air, weaving a spell of enchantment and horror. The visitors, their initial excitement turning to dread, began to realize the true nature of the mansion. The gadgets and cameras, once tools of the curious, now recorded scenes of terror and disbelief.

One by one, they found themselves facing the manifestations of the mansion's dark legacy. Some faced the Sphinx's riddles, their answers a matter of life or death. Others felt the icy touch of the Wendigos, their breaths turning to frost as despair set in. And still others looked into the unblinking eyes of the Basilisk, their screams silenced by the cold embrace of stone.

By the time the sun rose again, the mansion had claimed its due. The cycle of allure and terror had spun anew, each visitor now a part of the mansion's ongoing saga. Their voices joined the eternal whispers in the walls, their fates a warning to those who might follow.

The mansion, sat, yet ever hungry, settled into a deceptive peace, its doors once again open, its rooms ready to welcome the next group of unwary visitors. The cycle of Ravenhill Mansion continued, as inevitable as the dawn, as endless as the night.

<u>Message from the Author:</u>

I hope you enjoyed this book, I love astrology and knew there was not a book such as this out on the shelf. I love metaphysical items as well. Please check out my other books:

-Life of Government Benefits

-My life of Hell

-My life with Hydrocephalus

-Red Sky

-World Domination:Woman's rule

-World Domination:Woman's Rule 2: The War

-Life and Banishment of Apophis: book 1

-The Kidney Friendly Diet

-The Ultimate Hemp Cookbook

-Creating a Dispensary(legally)

-Cleanliness throughout life: the importance of showering from childhood to adulthood.

-Strong Roots: The Risks of Overcoddling children

-Hemp Horoscopes: Cosmic Insights and Earthly Healing

- Celestial Hemp Navigating the Zodiac: Through the Green Cosmos

-Astrological Hemp: Aligning The Stars with Earth's Ancient Herb

-The Astrological Guide to Hemp: Stars, Signs, and Sacred Leaves

-Green Growth: Innovative Marketing Strategies for your Hemp Products and Dispensary

-Cosmic Cannabis

-Astrological Munchies

-Henry The Hemp

-Zodiacal Roots: The Astrological Soul Of Hemp

- **Green Constellations: Intersection of Hemp and Zodiac**

-Hemp in The Houses: An astrological Adventure Through The Cannabis Galaxy

-Galactic Ganja Guide
Heavenly Hemp
Zodiac Leaves
Doctor Who Astrology
Cannastrology
Stellar Satvias and Cosmic Indicas
<u>Celestial Cannabis: A Zodiac Journey</u>
AstroHerbology: The Sky and The Soil: Volume 1
AstroHerbology:Celestial Cannabis:Volume 2
Cosmic Cannabis Cultivation
The Starry Guide to Herbal Harmony: Volume 1
The Starry Guide to Herbal Harmony: Cannabis Universe: Volume 2
Yugioh Astrology: Astrological Guide to Deck, Duels and more
Nightmare Mansion: Echoes of The Abyss

Check out my Virtual dispensary for all your hemp needs: https://shift.store/sg1fan23477/retail
If you want solar for your home
go
here: https://www.harborsolar.live/apophisenterprises/
Instagrams:
@apophis_enterprises,
@hempkingdom2024,
@apophisbookemporium,
@apophisfashion,
@apophisscardshop
Twitter: @apophisenterpr1,
Tiktok:@apophisenterprise
Youtube: @sg1fan23477
Podcast:ApophisChatZone: https://open.spotify.com/show/5zXbrCLEV2xzCp8ybrfHsk?si=fb4d4fdbdce44dec
Newsletter: https://apophiss-newsletter-27c897.beehiiv.com/